Waiting for a Warbler

Written by **Sneed B. Collard III**

Illustrated by **Thomas Brooks**

TILBURY HOUSE PUBLISHERS

"Do you think any birds will nest here this year?"
Nora asks, her breath misting in the crisp spring air.

"If they find what they're looking for,"
Owen answers.

"I hope they do," Nora says.
"Especially a sky-blue bird."

Owen laughs. "You mean
a Cerulean Warbler?"

"Yeah, that one."

"They're really rare. We only saw one of them
last year—and it was just passing through."

"I know. But maybe it will stay longer this year."

Thousands of miles to the south, the tropical forests begin to stir. From Peru and Colombia, all the way through Panama, Costa Rica, and southern Mexico, thousands of birds are getting ready. Millions of birds.

"We've done a good job here," Dad says, joining Owen and Nora. "We left our big old oaks and hickories on the property."

"And we also put in other native plants," adds Owen.

Dad smiles. "Thanks to you."

Improving their yard was Owen's idea. He had read how most people fill their yards with exotic plants—those that come from other places and provide little food for native insects and birds. Owen and his family have worked to plant native trees and shrubs instead.

Their efforts have begun to pay off.

"We saw more birds and butterflies last year than we ever did before," Dad says.

Owen reaches out and touches the tender tip of a dogwood branch. "I'll bet this year will be even better."

By early March, the birds are
on the move, beginning the
journey to their northern
breeding grounds. Some hug the
coastline along Central America
and Mexico. Others follow the
mountain ranges. One evening
in early April, as the sun flashes
its last rays over misty slopes in
Mexico, an especially large flock
of birds sets off directly north.
Their journey will be the
most dangerous of all.

American
Robin

Northern
Cardinal

Carolina
Wren

Red-bellied
Woodpecker

Northern
Mockingbird

Downy Woodpecker

Scarlet Tanager

White-eyed Vireo

Every morning over breakfast,
Owen and Nora watch their yard. They spot birds they see all
winter—robins, cardinals, wrens, mockingbirds, woodpeckers. As
the days grow longer and warmer, other birds begin showing up.

"Look, there's a White-eyed Vireo," Owen says. "And that's a Scarlet Tanager!"

Nora points. "What's that
bird on the branch?"

Owen focuses his binoculars.

"Hmm . . . some kind of flycatcher.

Least Flycatcher

See how it darts out to catch something
and then returns to its perch?"

The large flight of birds heads straight across the Gulf of Mexico. One of the birds is a male Cerulean Warbler. This is the first year he will try to find a mate and raise his own family. But first he must cross six hundred miles of open ocean. Along the way, he will find no islands on which to rest or feed. His muscles will burn so much energy that he'll lose half his body weight. Even if all goes well, it will take him eighteen hours to cross the water.

As each day passes, more leaves burst from their buds. Flowers bloom on the native trees and shrubs Owen and his family have planted.

As migrating birds pass through their yard. Owen and Nora keep journals of what they see.

"Look at this fat green caterpillar!" Nora exclaims as they walk around their property.

Owen begins sketching the insect. "That will make a juicy meal for a baby bird," he says.

Nora wrinkles her nose. "Yuck. I'll stick with strawberries."

The Cerulean Warbler and other birds cruise
a thousand feet above the waves. As they fly,
they make short flight calls to other birds. These
squeaky chirps sound very different from their
normal songs. They keep the flock together.
They exclaim, "We are alive. We can do it."

Halfway through their journey, however, the Cerulean and other birds feel a shift in the wind. When they left Mexico, tailwinds helped carry them northward, but now the winds begin to push against them. What the birds don't realize is that they are about to face their worst nightmare—a storm moving directly across their path.

"Come see this," Dad calls to Owen and Nora. The kids hurry into the living room.

"A large storm is swirling across the northern Gulf of Mexico," a TV weather woman says. "It will bring strong winds and heavy flooding all along the Gulf Coast."

Mom frowns. "That can't be good for the birds."

Owen feels his stomach clench. *Will the birds make it through?*

As the birds approach the
storm, the wind grows stronger.
Lightning splits the sky and
rain pummels the flock. The
Cerulean struggles to keep
flying. His speed drops, and his
muscles burn twice as much
energy as usual. All around him,
other warblers also struggle.

Daylight comes, but storm clouds blot out the sun. The birds have been flying for eighteen hours now, with no land in sight. Weaker birds use up the last of their reserves and fall into the stormy seas. Other birds keep flying. They claw at the wind, fighting to stay above the deadly waves. The Cerulean is one of them.

At school that morning, Owen gives a talk about migrating birds. "Some birds have already arrived," he tells his class. "Some will stay to nest, but others are heading to breeding grounds in Canada and Alaska."

"Are more birds on their way?" one girl asks.

"I hope so," Owen replies. "Especially the little birds called wood warblers. Our area is a final destination for many of them.

"They take advantage of the spring and summer explosion of insects here. The insects provide the birds with enough fat and protein to lay eggs and raise their chicks."

"Owen, how long will the warblers stay?" his teacher asks him.

"Only three or four months. Then they'll head back to Central and South America."

But only if they make it here first!

By now, the Cerulean and other warblers have been flying almost twenty-four hours. As they weaken and use the last of their energy, the birds sink closer and closer to the deadly waves. The Cerulean fights for his life.

Then, just before sunset, he spots a dark line through the torrential rain.

Land!

Pushing his body to its limit, he flaps toward the dark line and . . .

. . . lands in a mulberry tree!

The tiny bird has used almost every bit of his energy.
He is more exhausted than he has ever been.

But he is alive!

A few days later, Owen sits with his binoculars and nature journal.

"Do you see any more warblers?" Dad asks. The previous day, Owen had spotted a Black-throated Blue Warbler and an American Redstart.

Black-throated Blue warbler

American Redstart

Nashville
Warbler

Owen points to his journal. "I just got a glimpse of a Nashville Warbler, but I think he is just passing through. I'm worried that the storm killed a lot of warblers."

His dad sighs. "I worry about that, too."

Then they hear a high trio of notes, followed by a faster trill. Owen trains his binoculars high in a tree.

"Nora! Quick!" he shouts into the house.

His sister hurries out to the porch. "What is it?"

Owen thrusts the binoculars into her hands. "Top of the tree," he says, pointing.

Nora focuses the binoculars. "The sky-blue bird!" she exclaims. "It came back!"

"Or maybe a different one," Owen says with a grin.

Owen and his family expect the Cerulean Warbler to keep heading north, but the bird sticks around. Every morning, they listen to its trilling call from the tall trees behind their house. One day they see a second Cerulean—a female.

"Maybe they'll start a family!" Nora exclaims.

Owen doesn't dare believe it. Once the Ceruleans pair off, however, the male spends less time singing and more time hunting for insects.

"I guess they're finding what they need here," Mom says.

"Of course they are," Nora answers.

The Ceruleans
hide their nest
among thick
leaves high in a
white oak tree.

Every day, though, Owen
and Nora glimpse the
two warblers scouring
the surrounding trees and
shrubs for insects.

When one grabs a caterpillar
or bug, it disappears back
into the top of the tree.

"Do you think they're feeding
babies?" Nora wonders.

"I hope so," says Owen.

One day in late June, Owen is reading in the backyard when he hears short, sharp chipping sounds. He looks up to see a very messy-looking gray bird sitting on a branch. Owen flips through his bird guide but can't figure out what he's looking at. He's never seen such a drab, frumpy creature. Then, suddenly, the mother Cerulean lands next to the bird and feeds it a fat green caterpillar.

The babies! Owen tells himself. *They've fledged!*

During the next weeks, Owen and Nora glimpse the Cerulean family several more times. The babies grow quickly and learn to hunt for themselves.

Then, in late July, the warblers disappear as suddenly as they arrived.

"Do you think they've flown south again?" Nora asks.

"Probably. They don't stay long."

"Just long enough to fatten up on insects and give their babies a head start," Nora says.

Owen nods. "What if something happens and they don't make it back next year?" he worries.

But Nora is
already imagining
the birds in the
tree next summer.

"They'll be back," she reassures her big brother. "They're smart birds—and from now on, they know that our yard is the *best* place to make sky-blue babies."

Author's Note

Waiting for a Warbler was inspired by a spring birding trip my son and I took to the Texas coast. During our visit, we saw a dozen kinds of warblers and more than seventy other bird species. On our last day there, a tremendous storm charged into the area, and the severe weather gave us a first-hand glimpse of the dangers faced by songbirds as they migrate north and south each year.

One bird we missed seeing was the Cerulean Warbler. As with many other warblers, Cerulean numbers have dropped in the past fifty years. Forest destruction in both North and South America has probably been the greatest factor. When healthy mature forests are turned into tree plantations, roads, and housing developments, the birds are deprived of the habitats they need to safely live and nest.

A first step in helping Cerulean Warblers and other birds is to learn more about them. Understanding what birds need helps us protect them. The following pages will help you get started in birding *and* becoming part of the solution for our planet's winged wildlife.

Be a Birder!

Almost everyone loves watching wild animals, and birds can be seen almost anywhere. Even if you live in a large city, chances are that you can spot wild birds just outside your door. Want to get started? You'll need two things:

- **A pair of binoculars**. Almost any pair will do, but if you have a birthday coming, you might ask for a pair that is not too heavy and has 10X—ten times—magnification. My favorite size is "10 X 42," which has a magnification of ten times and front openings that are 42 millimeters wide. If you have trouble getting a pair, call your local library or a nature center and ask if they have any you can borrow.

- **A field guide of birds for your region—or one for North America**. Popular field guides include those published under the names of National Geographic, Peterson, and Kenn Kaufman. My son and I use *The Sibley Guide to Birds* more than any other, but almost any guide from a library or bookstore will work.

With binoculars and field guide in hand, it's time to find some birds! Even from your window, you should be able to see at least a couple of kinds. It's more fun, though, to explore a nearby park or other open space. When you see a bird, stop and focus your binoculars on it. Ask yourself some questions:

* How big is the bird?

* What color is it?

* What is the bird doing? Is it sitting on the ground, or up in a tree, or on a building? How high?

* What shape is its beak, or bill?

* Is it making any songs or calls?

Once you've observed the bird for a few moments, start flipping through your field guide. Don't be overwhelmed by the number of birds in the book. In the beginning, just skim through the pages until you find some that look similar to the one you are seeing. Some birds are easier to figure out than others. You may quickly learn to identify American Robins, House Sparrows, Rock Pigeons, Northern Mockingbirds, and American Crows. Use these "basic birds" to build your knowledge of other, more challenging birds.

One thing that will make your birding more rewarding is to carry a small notebook and colored pencils so that you can draw pictures of the birds you see and take notes about them. My son and I also take cameras.

If you like to keep a record of the birds you've seen, consider starting an eBird account. This is a free and wonderful online way to learn about the birds in your area and where to find them. Learn more at ebird.org.

Remember: *Have fun*! Don't worry if your friends learn birds faster than you. It's not a competition. Just help each other and enjoy it. Soon, you will start noticing birds everywhere you look. That will tell you that you have caught the birding bug!

Help Protect Birds

As you can tell from the story, it can be tough to be a bird. Birds face many threats—but there are things you can do to help them. Start by *keeping your cat indoors*. Bird researchers estimate that household and feral (wild) cats kill between *one and two billion birds* each year. By keeping kitty indoors, you make the lives of songbirds a lot easier.

Another thing you can do is *plant native perennials, shrubs, and trees around your house or yard*—just like Owen's family did. Warblers and many other songbirds migrate north because they find an explosion of insects here every spring. Birds need these fat, juicy insects to feed and raise their babies. Insects, though, need native plants to live and reproduce.

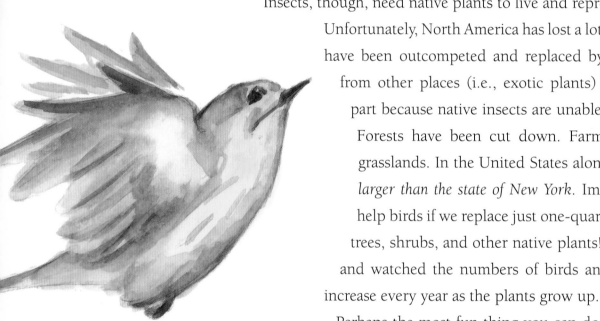

Unfortunately, North America has lost a lot of its native plants. Many have been outcompeted and replaced by invasive plants—plants from other places (i.e., exotic plants) that multiply rapidly, in part because native insects are unable to eat and control them. Forests have been cut down. Farms have replaced natural grasslands. In the United States alone, *our lawns cover an area larger than the state of New York.* Imagine how much we can help birds if we replace just one-quarter of our lawn areas with trees, shrubs, and other native plants! My family has done this and watched the numbers of birds and butterflies in our yard increase every year as the plants grow up.

Perhaps the most fun thing you can do to help birds is to join a group such as your local Audubon Society chapter. Audubon Society groups conduct field trips, classes, and other activities that help people learn about and protect birds. For more about the Audubon Society, visit them at www.audubon.org. Among the features you'll find there is a tool to help you choose bird-friendly plants for your yard.

Two other groups my family and I belong to are the American Birding Association (www.aba.org) and The Cornell Lab of Ornithology (www.birds.cornell.edu). Both organizations promote bird education and conservation and are great ways to increase your knowledge of some of earth's most fascinating creatures.

For everything you do, the birds will thank you.

Learning More

Many great bird books for young people have appeared in the past few years. Here are a few:

Tiny Bird: A Hummingbird's Amazing Journey, by Robert Burleigh (Henry Holt, 2020)

Beaks!, by Sneed B. Collard III (Charlesbridge, 2002)

Fire Birds—Valuing Natural Wildfires and Burned Forests, by Sneed B. Collard III (Bucking Horse Books, 2015)

Birds of Every Color, by Sneed B. Collard III (Bucking Horse Books, 2019)

Numenia and the Hurricane: Inspired by a True Migration Story, by Fiona Halliday (Page Street Kids, 2020)

The Nest That Wren Built, by Randi Sonenshine (Candlewick, 2020)

A Place for Birds, by Melissa Stewart (Peachtree, 2015)

Two adult books that are great references for your parents and teachers are:

Nature's Best Hope: A New Approach to Conservation That Starts in Your Yard (2020) and *Bringing Nature Home: How You Can Sustain Wildlife with Native Plants* (2009), both by Douglas W. Tallamy

To learn more about bird conservation and specific birds, also check out these websites:

All About Birds (Cornell Lab of Ornithology)
https://www.allaboutbirds.org/news/

American Bird Conservancy
https://abcbirds.org/

The Peregrine Fund
https://peregrinefund.org/

BirdLife International
http://www.birdlife.org/

For the real Nora and Owen.
—Love, Uncle Sneed

To my parents, for paving a path
alive with birds and brushstrokes.
—Thomas

Text © 2021 by Sneed B. Collard III
Illustrations © 2021 by Thomas Brooks

Hardcover ISBN 978-0-88448-852-1

Tilbury House Publishers
Thomaston, Maine
www.tilburyhouse.com

Library of Congress Control Number: 2020947538

Designed by Frame25 Productions
Printed in China

10 9 8 7 6 5 4 3 2 1

Sneed B. Collard III has written more than eighty-five award-winning books for young people including *Beaks!, Catching Air: Taking the Leap with Gliding Animals*, and the mystery chapter book *The Governor's Dog is Missing*. He and his son, Braden, began birding together in 2014 and since then have seen almost one thousand species of birds in North and South America, Asia, Europe, and the Middle East. They continue to bird with their "bird dog" Lola, and often write about their adventures in their blog, FatherSonBirding.com. To learn more about Sneed or how to invite him to your school for an author visit, writing workshop, or birding field trip, contact him through his website, www.sneedbcollardiii.com.

Thomas Brooks illustrates natural history and wildlife subjects in a variety of mediums, with a focus on combining digital and traditional methods of image making. He has been an exhibit artist and scientific illustrator for several regional parks and nature centers and loves projects that combine education and fine art. This is his debut picture book.